GRANDAD'S
PRAYERS
OF THE
EARTH

For my Grandad,
D.W. Wilton,
and for grandparents
and grandchildren
everywhere who listen for the
prayers of the earth.

With special thanks to Liz Bicknell,
for her warmth and wisdom
and gentle editing.

D.W.

———

For Aidan and Vicente

With special thanks to Eoin Keating,
Darren McCormack, and Brian de Salvo.

P.J.L.

Text copyright © 1999 by Douglas Wood
Illustrations copyright © 1999 by P.J. Lynch

All rights reserved.

First edition 1999

Library of Congress Cataloging-in-Publication Data
Wood, Douglas, date.
Grandad's prayers of the earth / Douglas Wood ;
illustrated by P.J. Lynch. —1st ed.
p.   cm.
Summary: Because Grandad has explained how all things in
the natural world pray and make a gift to the beauty of life, his
grandson is comforted when Grandad dies.
ISBN 0-7636-0660-X
[1. Prayers—Fiction.   2. Death—Fiction   3. Nature—Fiction.
4. Grandfathers—Fiction]   1. Lynch, Patrick James, ill.
II. Title.
PZ7.W84738Gr   1999
[Fic]—dc21   98-47805

2 4 6 8 10 9 7 5 3 1

Printed in Italy

This book was typeset in Oxalis.
The illustrations were done in watercolor.

Candlewick Press
2067 Massachusetts Avenue
Cambridge, Massachusetts 02140

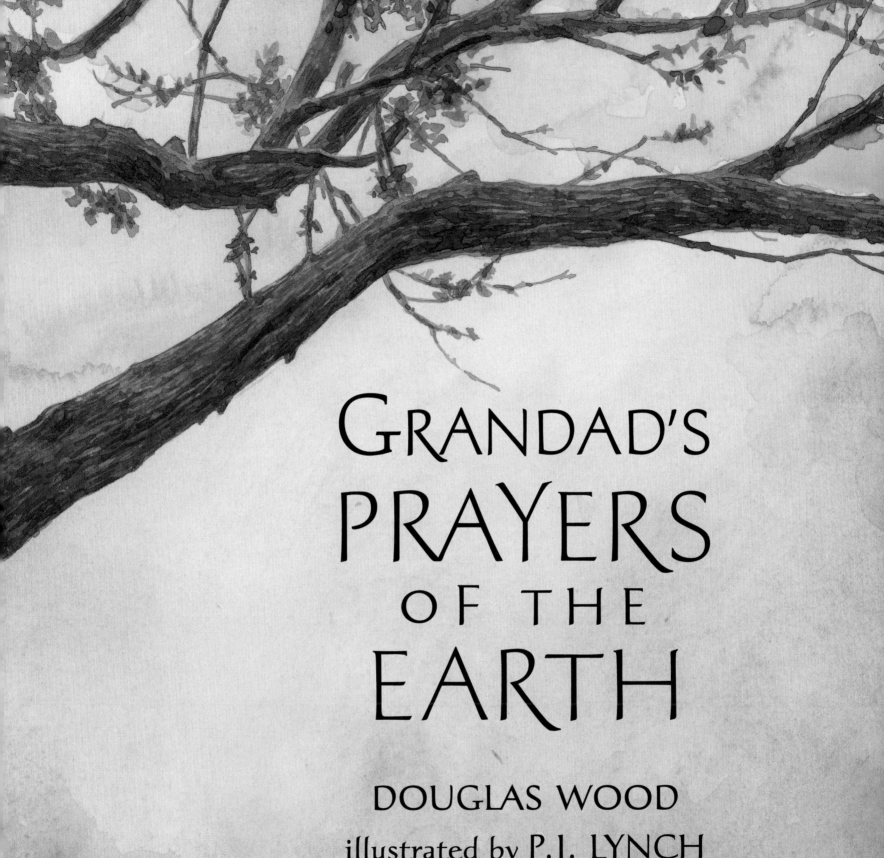

GRANDAD'S
PRAYERS
OF THE
EARTH

DOUGLAS WOOD

illustrated by P.J. LYNCH

CANDLEWICK PRESS
CAMBRIDGE, MASSACHUSETTS

When I was little, my Grandad was my best friend. Being with him always made the world seem just right.

Grandad and I liked to go for walks in the woods together. We didn't walk very far. Or very fast. Or very straight.

While we walked, I would ask him questions about things I wasn't sure of.

"Why is it, Grandad . . . ?" I would ask. And "What if . . . ?" And "Does it ever . . . ?"

One day I asked my Grandad about prayers.

For a long time,
Grandad was quiet.
He didn't say anything
until we came to the
tallest trees in the forest.
And then he answered
with a question.

"Did you know, boy,"
he whispered,
"that trees pray?"

I listened closely, but
I couldn't hear them.

"See how they reach
for the sky," he said.
"They reach and reach—
for clouds and sun
and moon and stars.
And what else is
reaching for heaven
but a prayer?"

I thought about the trees and kept listening for them, and while I thought I sat down on an old, mossy rock.

"Rocks pray, too," said Grandad. "Pebbles and boulders and old weathered hills. They are still and silent, and those are two important ways to pray."

I thought hard about the rocks. I picked up a pebble and stuck it in my pocket.

We walked a little farther and came to a small stream. The water splashed and sparkled, and tiny fish hovered in the shadows.

"Do streams pray, too, Grandad?" I asked.

"Streams pray, too," he answered. "And lakes and rivers and waters of all kinds. Sometimes they pray silently, like the rocks. They lie still and calm, reflecting clouds or birds or sunsets or the first evening star.

"Sometimes they pray with movement, flowing across the face of the earth, giving themselves to the ocean, giving themselves to the sky, and beginning their journey all over again.

"Sometimes waters pray with laughter, chuckling to their friends the rocks, and sometimes they pray by dancing, leaping into the air and falling back again.

"These are all ways
to pray," said Grandad,
"but there are more.

"The tall grass prays as
it waves its arms beneath
the sky, and flowers pray
as they breathe their
sweetness into the air.

"The wind prays as it
whispers and moans
and sighs. It is saying
a prayer and singing a
hymn at the same time.

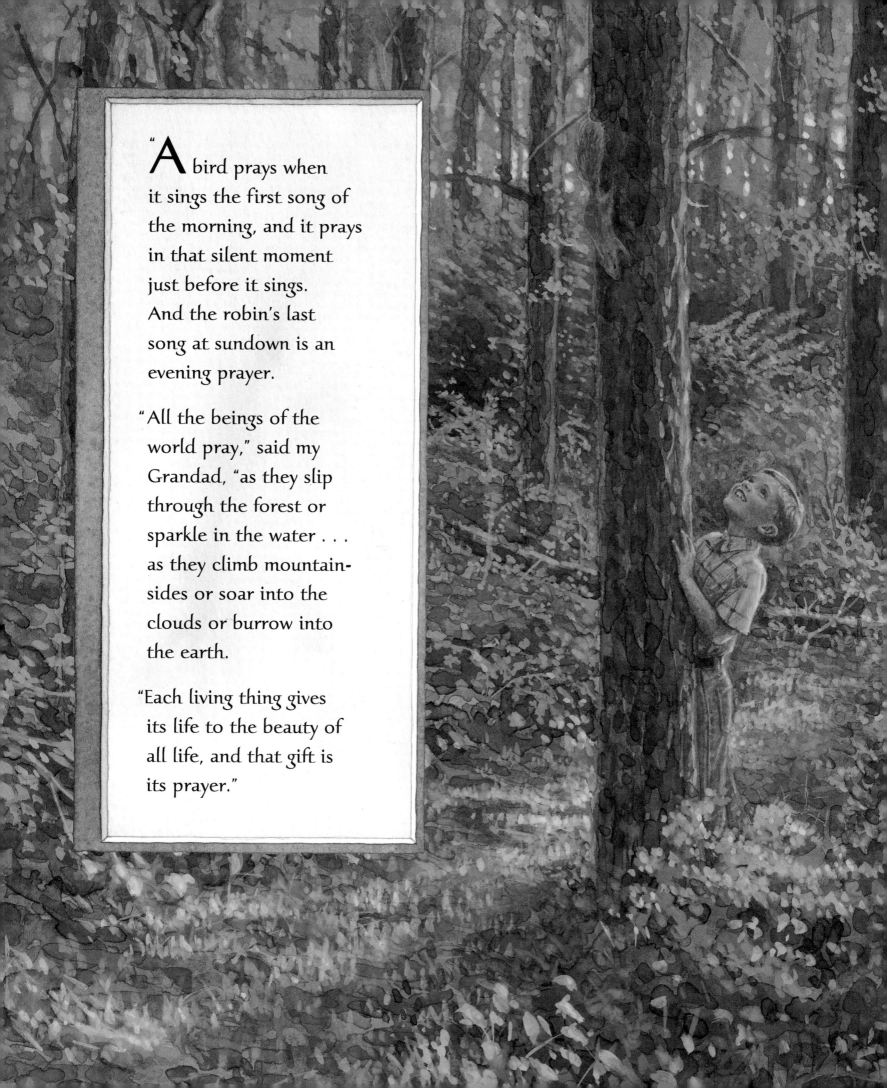

"A bird prays when it sings the first song of the morning, and it prays in that silent moment just before it sings. And the robin's last song at sundown is an evening prayer.

"All the beings of the world pray," said my Grandad, "as they slip through the forest or sparkle in the water . . . as they climb mountain-sides or soar into the clouds or burrow into the earth.

"Each living thing gives its life to the beauty of all life, and that gift is its prayer."

Then we were quiet,
my Grandad and I. He
was watching something
far away, and I was
thinking about all he
had said, about rocks
and trees and grass
and birds and flowers.
Finally I asked him to
tell me about the prayers
of people.

Grandad smiled and
ruffled my hair.
"People pray some of
the most wonderful
prayers of all," he said.

"Bending down to smell
a flower can be a prayer,"
said my Grandad.

"Quietly watching the
sunrise, feeling the slow
turning of the earth
and saying hello to a
new day is one of the
oldest prayers.

"Standing in a snowy woods
on a winter day and
watching your breath
become part of the
breath of the world is
a way to pray.

"Making music or painting
a picture can be a prayer.

"Holding hands around the table with family and friends, remembering all that holds us together and giving thanks is one of the greatest prayers.

"Sometimes," said Grandad, "people pray when they are sad or sick or lonely, or have a problem too big to carry by themselves. They may say words they have learned from their fathers or mothers or grandads or great-grandmothers. But often they must find their own words. The important thing to remember is that the words will always be right if they are real and true and come from the heart."

We had walked far enough and Grandad said it was time to go back, but I had one last question.

"Are our prayers answered, Grandad?" I asked.

Grandad smiled. "Most prayers are not really questions," he said. "And if we listen very closely, a prayer is often its own answer. Like the trees and winds and waters, we pray because we are here—not to change the world, but to change ourselves.

"Because it is when we change ourselves . . . that the world is changed."

My Grandad and I went for many walks after that one, and I often listened for the prayers of the earth, but was never sure I heard them.

Then one day, my
Grandad was gone.
And no matter how
hard I prayed, he didn't
come back. He couldn't
come back.

I prayed and prayed
and prayed until I
couldn't pray anymore.

And so I didn't,
for a long time.

And the world seemed
    dark and lonely without
        my Grandad in it.

Until one day I went
for a walk. I found a big
rock under some tall
trees and sat down on it.
Overhead the branches
swayed and a breeze
whispered in the leaves.
I heard a stream flowing
nearby, and a robin singing
from a honeysuckle bush.

And I heard something
else, too—something
in the sounds of breezes
and birds and water.
I heard prayers.

The earth was praying,
just like my Grandad said.

So I joined in.

"Thank you," I prayed,
"for tall trees and sweet
flowers, for still rocks
and singing birds
and especially . . .
for my Grandad."

And as I prayed,
something changed,
and my Grandad
seemed somehow near.

And for the first time
in a long time,
the world seemed
just right.